Contents

Chapter 1
The Hairy Bikers

Have you heard of the After School Club? Not the place you go when your mum and dad can't pick you up after school. I mean the gang. Everyone else calls them the Hairy Bikers, because they wear leather jackets. It's not a very funny nick-name.

At first I told myself *you don't want to join any clubs, Sam. Who wants to hang around after school?* I mean, really, this place is a dump. I haven't got any friends and I'm not really into clubs or teams. I thought it would all be rubbish. But sometimes you just have to give things a go.

****

Everyone thinks the Hairy Bikers are weird. They do look a bit freaky, apart from Lena, who is cool. But they're not bullies like Tom's gang. You don't want to run into those guys if you can help it.

I bumped into Tom one day. My foot skidded and I slipped. It was no big deal. But he made it one.

"Hey, loser, get out the way!"

"I'm not in your way."

"Yeah? Well, I say you are."

He came right up to me. His chin was right in my face. I didn't want to back down so I just stood my ground and tried to look hard.

"I don't think you heard me," he said with a sneer. "What do you reckon, lads?"

Three ugly lads came over to me. They were big, with fists like bricks. I was cornered.

"What's the matter, loser, cat got your tongue?" he said.

I was about to answer back. I couldn't fight all of them, but I'd try.

Then someone said, "What's the problem?"

It was a new voice, one of the Hairy Bikers.

Tom's eyes flashed. He looked angry, but jumpy too. "It's nothing to do with you," he snapped.

"What if I say it is?" The Biker smiled.

Tom looked from me to the Biker, who was joined by Lena and two other boys. He shrugged.

"You're not worth it," he said to me, and left in a hurry, taking his bullies with him. I'd never seen him look afraid of anyone before.

I wanted to say something. To let the Bikers know that I can fight my own battles.

6

But all that came out was, "Thanks." By then it was too late. They had gone.

I didn't think about them again, not really. It's not like I wanted to be a part of their gang or anything.

But then one day Lena spoke to me. She asked me to join the club, and after that nothing was ever the same again.

****

Lena is so cute. How could I say no? I just stood there smiling like I was stupid. I must have looked like the cat that got the cream. No wonder she smiled back!

"We don't do much at the after school club," she said. We just, you know, hang about."

"It sounds ... fun."

She shrugged. "If you're up for it I'll meet you by the changing rooms at 7."

If I was up for it? Oh boy, was I up for it!

****

She turned up late, but I knew she would.
Lena is not the kind of girl who is early.
Lena keeps you waiting, and you don't mind.

"Sorry, Sam, got held up." She was out of
breath. "Come on, you can meet the other
guys."

"Great," I said, but I didn't mean it. I
hate meeting people. I never know what to
say, so I think it's better to say nothing at
all.

She took me to the sports field. There
they were – a line of boys in leather jackets.

"This is Spud, and this is Luke," she said nodding to a tall boy with a shaved head, and a shorter boy with thick, untidy blond hair. "That's Benno there, with the white streaks in his hair."

I'd met him when I had that run-in with Tom. He was the one who stood up for me.

"And you know me."

I nodded and tried to look like I was hard. First rule of joining any club is to look as if you hate the world and everyone in it. Lena put a hand on my arm and I bit my lip. Her red hair hung down her back. It looked so soft in the light of the full moon.

"Where are your bikes?" I asked. I don't know why I opened my mouth. They just laughed and rolled their eyes.

"You didn't fall for all that Hairy Bikers rubbish?" asked Spud.

"No," I said with a sniff. "But it does seem stupid to have a name if it's not true."

"Who said it isn't true?" grinned Benno.

"Well, I can't see any bikes!"

"That doesn't mean a thing. We could have them stored away somewhere," said Spud.

Benno looked at his friends. "Come on, lads. Why don't we give him a break? Let's show him."

"Show me what?" I asked.

"The real deal."

Lena yawned and moved closer.

"The truth is ... we are the Hairy Bikers," she said as she sniffed my neck.

Then she turned to the others. "You know, he really does smell yummy."

The boys stood round me in a circle and licked their lips.

"What are you doing?"

They were acting weird.

"What we always do," Spud laughed.
"We're going to hunt you down ..."

Chapter 2
Waiting in the Dark

"Ha ha, very funny!" I said. I grinned.

But they didn't grin back. They moved towards me in a circle. Benno put his head on one side and let out a funny sort of screech.

"What's going on?" I was getting ready – something bad was coming. I knew I couldn't fight them, but I would do my best.

Then it happened. Something hit me from behind. Something with claws that sank into my neck. I fell forwards. When I rolled over they had gone. They had left me. I rubbed my head and my neck. My hand felt wet and when I looked at it I could see blood. My blood.

"Losers!" I shouted. But no one answered. The playing fields were empty and the Hairy Bikers had vanished. So much for after school clubs. So much for Lena liking me. It had all been a stupid game. But they would pay. I would show them. I'm not afraid of anyone.

****

"You coming tonight?"

It was the next day and Lena was whispering in my ear. How dare she? I wanted to shout at her. To shake her. But when I looked into her green eyes the words vanished.

"It's OK, you know. The boys are always like that at first, but they get better." She hooked an arm in mine.

"They didn't seem to want me around."

"Oh, they do. They just have a funny way of showing it. Anyone new always has a hard time."

I raised an eyebrow. "Anyone new?"

"Yes, we've had a few come and go."

She tugged my arm lightly. "Oh, come on. Give it another go. Show the guys that you're not that easy to scare."

"I'm not," I said. "OK, I'll be there."

Lena grinned. "Cool. See you later."

****

I wasn't afraid of them. I would show Lena that I was just as hard as her friends. I could take them on. All of them. I stood there on the playing field. I felt good.

Strong. Stronger than I'd felt for a long time. And I wasn't afraid. Really I wasn't.

I waited and waited. My hands were clenched shut. I watched a magpie land at my feet and peck at my trainers. I saw the care-taker shouting at two stray dogs in the bike sheds. He waved a stick at them, but that just made them bark louder.

I stood still. I listened to every sound. They would not sneak up on me this time. But they never came.

I waited for two hours. I waited until it was so dark that I couldn't see the field any more. Then I went home.

I was almost at my door when I heard a sound.

"Gotcha!" I yelled. My hands were in the air ready to hit out. But it was only a fox. A small ragged fox, with sharp teeth that gleamed. It was sitting at my feet.

"Get lost!" I snapped, and went inside.

Chapter 3
Running Away

The next day at school Lena wouldn't look at me. She blanked me! As if I'd been the one that hadn't turned up. I was so angry I could have spat at her. I was sick of the Hairy Bikers and their silly games. Sick of it all. My head hurt and my eyes were stinging. I felt shivery and cold. But most of all I was hungry. Really hungry.

By afternoon break I was ready to go home. And I would have done too, if it hadn't been for the school care-taker. I could hear him shouting. The sound came from the bike sheds. I crept towards the door and looked in. He was beating a stray dog with a stick. It was one of the dogs I'd seen before. The animal was on its back on the floor, shaking.

"Stupid filthy mutt!" he yelled. The stick made a 'thwacking' noise as it hit the dog's belly.

"Stop it!" I yelled and ran towards him. I grabbed the stick and threw it away.

The care-taker raised his hand but I grabbed hold of it. I pushed him and ran for the door. But I couldn't leave the dog. I turned back. It was gone.

Where was it? How could it vanish like that? There was no time to wonder. I had to run. My belly was growling and the care-taker was shouting. I had to get away.

I ran towards the field. Ran so fast that I couldn't see. The grass was a blur of green. The trees zipped past me. My belly was still growling. Over and over. On and on. The sound was so loud. It felt like a rocket inside. Like I was howling at the top of my voice. And I was! I was wailing. I felt wild and free. Running like the wind, away from the school. Away from everything. Running until my foot twisted on a stone and I fell, head first into the dirt.

"Are you OK?" Lena was standing above me. She offered a hand.

"Where did you come from?" I asked.

"Never mind."

"I thought you weren't talking to me," I said.

"I thought it was the other way around."

I opened my mouth to speak, but she shook her head and pulled me up. "It's OK," she said. "I know it's hard. I know what it's like."

"What?"

"When you become a part of our club, it feels funny at first."

"I don't know what you're talking about."

"Yes you do." She jabbed me with her finger. "You feel it too, the need to run away from it all." She laughed. "I saw you. I heard you howling."

"I wasn't howling."

"If you say so. I heard what you did with the dog."

"What do you mean?"

She smiled. "You saved it."

"How do you know that? Who told you?"

"Doesn't matter."

I scratched my head. This was crazy. How could she know about the dog already? It had only happened minutes ago, and no one else had been there.

"We're meeting again tonight. Do you want to come?"

I should have said no, but my head hurt. I was tired, and so very hungry. I just wanted everything to go away.

"OK, I'll come."

"You won't be sorry," Lena said.

Then she was gone.

Chapter 4
Join the Club

I waited by the bike sheds. I could see
the field and the changing rooms. I could
see the school too. It looked creepy in the
dark. Like an empty shell.

I spotted Lena first. She ran towards me.
She was smiling and her red hair was tied
up in a pony tail.

"You came!" she said.

"Yes, I said I would."

"I wouldn't have blamed you if you hadn't."

From across the field I saw two bikes racing. Spud and Luke.

"So you do have bikes?"

Lena grinned. "Yes, just not motor bikes."

Then Benno got there. He was pushing his bike. He leaned it against the wall of the changing rooms.

34

"Sam! Good to see you, mate."

Mate? They were being friendly. There had to be a catch.

"I heard what you did," Benno said. "That was good of you."

"What?"

"The dog and the care-taker. Lena told me."

"Erm, I didn't really do anything," I said.

"That's not what I've been told." He looked at Spud. "We weren't joking around with you the other night. We really are the Hairy Bikers. You see ... we have a secret."

"It's best if we show him," said Lena.

"Show me what?"

She stepped back and closed her eyes. The air shimmered around her and then there was a popping sound in my ears. I watched as she got smaller and smaller. Her face stretched and her skin became furry. And then … then she was a fox! A small ragged fox.

"What the – "

"Don't be scared," said Benno. "We can all do it. Watch."

He pointed to Spud and Luke. They waved and then they changed. Just like Lena. The air shimmered and fizzed, and then they were dogs. Dogs I had seen before. One of them trotted towards me. It was the one I'd saved from the care-taker.

It all made sense now. The night I'd been waiting for them. They had been here after all. They'd just been different!

"And you, what do you turn into?" I
asked.

Benno smiled. "I'm a magpie. You saw
me the other night."

Pecking at my trainers. Of course!

"I don't know what to say. How did you all get this way?"

"The same way as you will," he said.

"Me? But I'm not like that!"

Benno tapped me on the arm. "You are. You said you wanted to join our club, didn't you?"

"Yes, but I didn't know what you were!"

"We're shape-shifters. We've been given a gift to change our shape to something else."

"But I'm *not like you*," I said again.

Benno smiled. "Remember the first night. Something hit you? It made you bleed? That's how the gift is passed on. But it has to be done on the night of a full moon, and to someone who wants to join our club."

"No ..."

"Look, mate, it's not so bad. It means that we're magic. That we can do stuff that other kids can't."

I could feel my legs shaking. My face was damp with sweat. The hunger was back.

"It means you're free, Sam. You can go anywhere and do anything. You can help people, or you can help yourself. It's up to you."

My legs gave out and I fell. My hands pressed into the grass. I wanted to cry. I wanted to wail. But most of all I wanted to run.

And so I did. On all fours. My skin turned to fur, and my hands became sharp claws. I could smell rain in the air. I could see so clearly, like everything was in 3D. I didn't feel it coming, but I had changed. I was a cat. A huge, wild-looking tom cat, with scars all over me and it felt ... great!

So now I'm a Hairy Biker. One of the weirdos. I don't have a bike, but I am hairy ... sometimes. It felt funny at first. But now I love it. I'm free. I can run and jump. I'm fast and strong. I've got friends and we're a team. We look out for each other. We also help other kids, outsiders, like us. We put things right. Fight the bad and stand up to the bullies like Tom.

I've always hated school, but now it's OK. Because I have a secret. I'm a member of the After School Club.

You can join too, if you want ...

Bomb!
by
Jim Eldridge

The clock is ticking ...
Rob's a top bomb disposal
expert. He has to defuse a
bomb in a school before
it's too late.
Can he do it?

Take Two
by
Jo Cotterill

Max asks Carla and her
best friend Lily to the
prom. Instead of getting
mad, they decide to get
even. It's sure to be a
night Max will never
forget!

Killer Croc
by
S. P. Gates

Levi is in danger. There's a killer croc on the loose – and it's hungry!

Can he escape its jaws?

Topspin
by
Sean Callery

Tim needs to learn the topspin serve to win the tennis final. But his dad is his tennis coach and he walks out on the family. Can Tim do it alone?

You can order these books directly from our website at
www.barringtonstoke.co.uk